JEFFREY
and
JASMINE

JEFFREY
and
JASMINE

Dealing With Not-So-Easy Dilemmas

JEAN LEE

authorHOUSE®

AuthorHouse™
1663 Liberty Drive
Bloomington, IN 47403
www.authorhouse.com
Phone: 1-800-839-8640

Published by AuthorHouse 12/01/2015

ISBN: 978-1-4918-4301-7 (sc)
ISBN: 978-1-4918-4302-4 (e)

Library of Congress Control Number: 2015909878

Print information available on the last page.

Any people depicted in stock imagery provided by Thinkstock are models, and such images are being used for illustrative purposes only. Certain stock imagery © Thinkstock.

This book is printed on acid-free paper.

Because of the dynamic nature of the Internet, any web addresses or links contained in this book may have changed since publication and may no longer be valid. The views expressed in this work are solely those of the author and do not necessarily reflect the views of the publisher, and the publisher hereby disclaims any responsibility for them.

This book is dedicated in loving memory to

Mom and Dad.

ACKNOWLEDGMENTS

I am most grateful to the Heavenly Father through Jesus Christ that this writing project has been completed.

Thanks to Evelyn Moore and Gwendolyn Robinson, colleagues, for serving as a sounding board during the inception of this project. I am indebted to Juene Parker and Sandra Fitzgerald, colleagues for their insightful inputs. Melinda Brown, Verdell Thompson and Lynette Byrom have offered encouragement and wisdom to keep the project moving. Thanks to my family members: my nephew, Lester, cousin, Alvin, sister, Margaret, sister-in-law, Leslie, and my brother, Lester—who did readings—offered their comments.

Dr. John Green's (Bos) and Ralph Dines' fascination with children's literature offered invaluable suggestions.

More importantly, thanks to the late Ronald Hill for his untiring, relentless support to the project completion. Karen and Keith McKenzie cheered me on. Benjamin Brookman shared his computer expertise. Lisa, my cousin, shared her viewpoint for embracing the need to express those characteristics: the positive driving forces in one's life as good.

The editor, Cassandra Franklin-Barbajosa, has been supportive and has brought a rich perspective to this project.

Thanks to the constant prayers of Theodora Thompson, LaVern Finks, Carmen Robinson, Wendell Watkins, Robert Henry, Gail Murray, Dorothy and Thaddeus Moore, Magdalene Fitzgerald and family, and countless others who helped to sustain me during this writing.

CHAPTER 1

Ironing Out the Community Wrinkles

Somerville, Maryland, at a glance, seems to hibernate like a groundhog that sleeps through winter. Somerville's unassuming manner reveals its special charm, like the gazebo in the landscaped town square where young and old gather to chat, play a game of chess, or just hang out. Many families move into the town, attracted by the Random Acts of Kindness Club, the Greatest Grandma Pageant, and the much-anticipated Pet Festival, featuring a melodious singing frog quartet, a daring twosome of goldfish that jump through hoops and play fast-moving soccer, and starring the popular acrobatic hamster performing rollover stunts. Daffodils accent the rectangular boxwoods, glossy evergreens, Japanese hollies, and yews. Red and gold barberries and splashes of blue-green junipers brighten the town garden, a colorful backdrop as parents haul cargos of squirming children to basketball camp and cheerleading sessions. Sharing rides give the families a chance to get to know each other better because all the children attend the same school.

On a beautiful Monday spring day in 1997, the *Somerville Community Gazette* sends out an announcement asking families to attend a special meeting at the Community Center at 7 p.m. on the following Saturday. Caroline Brown calls Lydia Jefferson—who lives across the street—to share theories about what the meeting could be about. They could only guess, so Lydia—who knows several people in the town administration office—decides to make a few calls to get to the bottom of such highly classified information. She promises Caroline that she would get back to her if she finds out why the meeting is so important. No one at the town office will leak anything about the urgent gathering. Curiosity is building up throughout the town but everybody has to wait. No exceptions!

As in so many small towns, parents catch up on tidbits of news at the grocery store, during short breaks from yard work, or when strolling after dinner to get some exercise. When the conversation gets around to their kids, the question frequently asked is, "Have you had to coax and prod your children to do their chores?" The resounding response is "YES!" And the common denominator is that the children are far too engrossed in their hand-held video games. Beds are unmade. Dishes are piled high. The trash container never makes it to the outside bin unless a parent steps in and completes the job.

This humble task is met with crankiness: "Why do *I* have to take out the trash?" Their whining way of expressing the opinion is that they should be absolutely free from such mundane responsibilities. As the parents share, they discover that they are not alone in coaxing and prodding them during this growing-up stage, affirming that OUR children are our lovable "apples of our eyes." "They'll understand once they have children of their own," says one parent, "and I'll just bet they'll come and tell us about it."

The obsession with hand-held video games—an innocent enough entertainment pastime on the surface—is beginning to wreak havoc from their unsuspecting presence that is creeping into people's lives and businesses of Somerville. Video games are left on the lawns and sidewalks. The Community Korner Store is starting to receive a barrage of calls about whether staff has found video games on the counters, inside snack racks, left in the refrigerator, and just about every place in the store. At home, they're lost under the couch and sitting on top of the washing machine. They're on the kitchen counter behind the salt-and-pepper shakers. They're everywhere!

*　　*　　*

Saturday night finally arrives. Every family appears to have shown up. Mayor Wendell Vandyke and his family moved to Somerville 15 years ago and came to know many of the people living there. He's the kind of man who helps you get the job done when you think you can't.

Mayor Vandyke thanks everyone for coming to the urgent meeting. The audience becomes suddenly silent, signifying that all eyes are focused on him. The mayor hesitates, then takes a deep breath and says, "We *can* find a solution." Everyone is puzzled but waits to hear what he's trying to say. "Reports from the Community Korner Store have bombarded my office about endless phone calls from Somerville children looking for misplaced video games, interrupting the daily flow of running the store," says the mayor.

Clearing his throat, Mayor Vandyke continues. "Postal carriers must tread carefully on tiptoes because they might trip over a video game unintentionally left on the lawn. The UPS personnel may accidentally step on one and possibly fall while trying to make a delivery. Bicyclists have had to skid around these little electronic gadgets left on the sidewalk. Harmless as it may seem, they're creating a lot of distress."

The mayor tries to cite another example when a mother interrupts, "My child is very careful with his video games!" The audience is becoming a little anxious.

The mayor is prepared for their responses. "We have come together . . . ."

Another parent raises her hand and says, "Some of us know that the video games are a problem at home, but we had no idea it was *this* bad! What can we do?"

Mayor Vandyke continues, "I *do* thank you for your comments! They're most valuable. We're one community. Even though we may not agree on everything, we are neighbors and can work together." The audience's mood calms as they listen to what the mayor reassures everyone that this concern can be resolved.

One parent waves her hand and voices a suggestion. "Our fifth and sixth graders should head up the committee to come up with possible solutions."

Before the mayor could ask for volunteers, 12-year-old Jeffrey Woods' arm—forced by his friend Victor Ortiz—pops into the air. Victor, playing around with Jeffrey, laughs. Jeffrey tries the same move on Victor, who is in his sixth-grade class. Now, both are trying to subdue their laughter. A moment later, two fifth graders raise their hands to become part of the committee. Beaming with pride, the audience gives them a standing ovation. The parents are surprised but pleased.

On Tuesday after school the newly formed committee of fifth and sixth graders meet at the Community Center. When the team comes together they initially feel that their rights are infringed upon, but they can't deny the fact that they all have contributed to what had begun to spill over into the lives of others. The committee goes around in circles for several minutes over the guidelines for video game use that would restore order and promote goodwill in the community.

"I don't know why we gotta do this?" protests fifth grader Eric Taylor, who begins to get cold feet.

"Think!" says Jeffrey. "It'll keep us from getting grounded and having all our privileges taken away. Now, let's stay focused."

"You always want to run everything," whines Yamuna Chopra, the other fifth grader.

"Wake up! Do you want to work together, or do you want our parents to take over?" snaps Victor.

"OK!" they both agree. "Let's work together."

Jeffrey asks Eric to use the chalkboard to write down constructive activities while monitoring the use of the video games that would benefit the whole family:

1. Select a team captain and co-captain for each street to check for videos on the lawns, steps, and sidewalks.

2. Encourage each other to keep a must-do list of the chores they don't *want* to do, such as washing dishes, sweeping the floor, vacuuming, and doing laundry.

3. Read a book before playing with a video game. Use a clock to monitor the time spent on the video game.

4. Select a month to present book reports that have captured their attention to the community.

5. Realize that it is better to think of others rather than trying to get their way all the time.

6. Get permission from the Community Korner Store to put a tall rectangular box labeled: LOST & FOUND VIDEOS HERE. A team captain collects and returns them to the owners.

They think these guidelines will help everyone to get along. When the community approves their suggestions, their flyer— Building the Community Through Cooperation—will be given to every family encouraging them to discuss the ways the committee's ideas will be carried out. Jeffrey is confident that he and his team have done a good job.

CHAPTER 2

Stuck in Sticky Situations

On a perfectly brilliant summer morning in the valley of Somerville, Jeffrey brushes every strand of his black wavy hair in place. Looking into the bathroom mirror, he checks to see if his hair on both sides looks the way he wants. He takes three fingers and smoothes the top of his hair. Then, turning a small mirror at an angle, he checks the back of his head, repeats the process, and smoothes the back of his hair with the same three fingers.

He smiles and says to himself, "Things are shaping up!" As he finishes brushing his hair, Jeffrey thinks back to the previous day when two of his best friends, Marcus Parker and Victor Ortiz, were all at the new Kool Ice Cream Parlor, the hottest spot for enjoying delicious cold sweets.

He treated everyone to his favorite dessert-ice cream sundaes - the most expensive dessert on the menu. His other best friend, Andre Cho, couldn't hang out with them because he had to go to the dentist. Marcus, Victor, and Andre have been Jeffrey's friends since kindergarten. Now, they are all basketball players on their school team.

Before leaving the parlor in the mall, Marcus suggested that they scout out the big sale at Bizzy Buy. As Marcus and Victor looked at the stereos, Jeffrey scanned the jewelry case of watches. In the newspaper advertisement section, he remembered seeing a watch that glows in the dark every hour. Jeffrey spotted the watch of his choice and asked the sales associate, who was pleasant and attentive to his questions, to show it to him. He also tried on several different kinds of watches.

Marcus and Victor searched the store and finally spotted Jeffrey in the watch department. They raced to see what had aroused their friend's interest. Time was flying, and they all left the store together.

* * *

Snapping out of his flashback, Jeffrey switches his thinking. He imitates the sounds and motions of an airplane, extending both hands to mimic the wings of the plane. He glides his feet and propels his wings, homing in on a final target. He makes a dive and lands his body in a crisscross position onto the soft target of his bed. While lying there, Jeffrey's thoughts pleasantly drift back to the watch he saw at Bizzy Buy.

Suddenly, he painfully remembers that the bill for those sundaes came to $17, swallowing up most of his $20 bi-weekly allowance.

After treating his friends, Jeffrey realizes the sad truth that he has committed a bad move: blowing his allowance! Then, his mind races forward to the community meeting. He remains bewildered that he is drafted for the Community Concerns Committee that can impact his relationship with the fellows on the basketball team. This is a worry he doesn't need right now. He sighs—drowning in the thought that when it rains, it pours—and wonders how something like this could happen to him.

Trying to recover from his allowance blunder, he imagines how that spectacular watch would look on him when, suddenly, his concentration is interrupted. Jasmine, his 8-year-old little sister, pops her head through the doorway of his bedroom and asks, "Whatcha doing?"

"Minding my own business and hoping that somebody else will do the same! Get the hint?"

Jasmine laughs. "I *know* the hint isn't for me!" She rushes over to hug her brother and soften his mood.

"Hey, Pumpkin! What do you want?"

Jasmine's playful expression changes to a more serious look. Reluctantly, she says, "Jeffrey, you have to promise to never tell Mom and Dad my secret. I'll get into serious trouble if they find out what I've done."

"Stop being so mysterious, and tell me!" Jeffrey says.

"Hold up!" says Jasmine and continues. "Well, I still have a little time before Grandma gets here," Jasmine says under her breath. Jeffrey, still puzzled, says in a deliberate tone, "You have five seconds to tell me, or vacate my room!"

Jasmine hesitates, but finally reaches a decision and says, "OK." She continues to search Jeffrey's face and checks his body language to see if he will listen. She feels at ease and quickly reveals what has been troubling her.

"Jeffrey, do you remember when Grandma gave me the beautiful single-pearl necklace to wear at my piano recital?" she asks.

"Yes, because you got it on the day I had basketball practice," he answers.

"The recital was scheduled for the next day, Friday," Jasmine recalls.

"Yeah, but where's this going, Jas?" Jeffrey interrupts. "Everyone was excited about your debut as a pianist. Grandma was really proud to have you wear the necklace she gave you. Wait a minute! Have you lost the necklace?!"

After a pause, Jeffrey prods. "I'm waiting for an answer, Jasmine."

Jasmine slowly nods her head.

Jeffrey mimics their mom, saying, "You know the rules of responsibility in caring for your things."

"How many times do I have to listen to those rules? I could scream, but I'm not!" Jasmine looks and feels frazzled.

Jeffrey glances at the clock on his dresser and gives his sister a timeout signal, reassuring her that he will help her search for the necklace. But first she must retrace her steps.

It's Saturday afternoon about 12:30 p.m., an hour before Jeffrey's basketball game with his friends at the neighborhood basketball court adjacent to the community center. Jeffrey tells Jasmine to speed it up a bit so that he isn't late. Before going to the community center, he has to complete one chore: clean his room before his mom inspects. He hugs Jasmine again.

Leaving her brother's room, Jasmine senses that Jeffrey's holding back what is bothering him. "I can tell you're up to something. Tell me about it soon," says the precocious little girl. "See you later, Jeff! Thanks!"

CHAPTER 3

Fessing Up

Jeffrey manages to clean his room in 15 minutes and leaves home to meet his friends for basketball. While walking to the community center, he tries to imagine what he could do to get that watch! He arrives at the basketball court 10 minutes earlier than his friends. His mind drifts back to the ways he has misused his allowance.

Jeffrey recalls the time he *had* to have his favorite basketball team's latest DVD. His grandparents had promised to get it by his birthday. Becoming a little impatient, he remembers that he couldn't wait. He cringes when he recalls that he had to take all the change from his robot bank—$6—and put it with his $20 allowance to get the DVD, which costs about $22.95, plus shipping.

In hindsight, he mumbles hard-to-understand undertones, "I couldn't wait for the sale, hum, hum, hum!" A voice interrupts his thinking. His friend, Marcus, skids in on his new sleek, black, racing bike.

"Hey, Marcus!" Jeffrey says, "Cool bike! You *love* those racers!"

"Yeah, you know I love bike racing, just like my Uncle Rick."

"So, what's up?" Jeffrey asks.

"Can't complain. Things are getting better. For a while, my parents grounded me because I was too much into my video games. I didn't complete my social studies research assignment. But I'm getting the message."

"I hear you!" Jeffrey agrees. "You gotta do what you gotta do!"

"Before I forget, let's remind Andre and Victor about joining the Math Club," says Marcus. "The deadline is soon."

"Yeah, it would be good for us to meet that deadline," Jeffrey agrees. "Be *sure* to tell Victor! You know how he is. He'll make sure we get it done." They both laugh.

"Man, have you heard the latest news?" Jeffrey asks. "Are you coming to the community meeting later this evening?"

Marcus confirms jokingly, with a hint of sarcasm. "The choice of going to the meeting is in no way mine. You know it's a family thing. I heard that you, Victor, and the committee are presenting."

"Look who's popping up!" Jeffrey yells, "The Committee Man!"

After running the distance to get to the game, Victor shows up gasping for breath. Andre jumps out of his dad's car. Within minutes, members of the other neighborhood team arrive, and a series of games begin.

Jeffrey's team is on a roll! He completes a 360-degree turn, dribbles the ball, fakes a pass, and seizes the opportunity to throw the ball to his teammate, Marcus, who is near the hoop and makes a slam-dunk. Andre snatches the opponents' ball. Then he dribbles and passes the ball through his legs to Victor, who dribbles as fast as lightning, fakes, and passes the ball to Jeffrey to shoot a three-pointer. The games are full of surprises, skill, and persistence.

Jeffrey's team has the winning edge! The other team has won the previous two games, so even this small victory is a boost. The opposing team is shocked that its rival executed such a brilliant game plan.

"You're on fire today!" shouts Big Tony Stanford from the other team.

"Yeah, we sure are!" Marcus laughs.

"That's for sure," Andre chimes in.

Jeffrey and his friends perform the standard rituals, exchanging fist bumps and sports lingo. "See you guys!" says Jeffrey. "Let's hook up soon for the next rivalry."

CHAPTER 4

Grappling to Find a Way

Jeffrey returns home with a grin on his face, extremely pleased about his team's victory. He enters his room and remembers to gather his clothing together for laundry. He's bored with doing the laundry, but he knows it has to be done.

To pep himself up for the dreaded chore, Jeffrey fakes a big smile while he robotically chants over and over: "These are my clothes. I am a responsible person. I am the man. I can do this."

Soon his dad will check out everything. He checks to see if Jeffrey sticks or strays from the schedule. With the clothes in the washer, Jeffrey goes back to his room. He reaches for the video game, but hesitates and chuckles, "I know I'm not going there." Then, he turns on the TV. Changing his mind, he quickly turns it off and begins to think some more about the desired treasure: the watch at Bizzy Buy. The community meeting quickly pops back in his mind; fortunately, *that* minor aggravation will soon come to an end. He switches back to thinking again about the watch.

"What can I *do*?" Jeffrey asks out loud. Jasmine pops her head in the doorway.

"Jeffrey, what was that outburst?"

Jeffrey shrugs his shoulders. "I'm just thinking out loud."

Jeffrey is hoping Jasmine will leave him alone. Like any sweet little sister, she loves to ask a lot of questions. When Jasmine hits him with a barrage of questions, it drives Jeffrey up a *WALL!*

"Thinking 'bout what? Something is bugging you, Jeff. What is it?" Jasmine continues to prod her brother.

"Ease up, Jas! I don't have to tell you everything I'm . . . ." Jeffrey hesitates, realizing his sister cares.

"There's a watch that I really want at Bizzy Buy," he confides. "If I had used my allowance in the right way, I could've had it by now." He's relieved to confess the regretful way he handled his allowance.

"You can come up with a way to make some more money," Jasmine states with confidence. "You can start your own business."

"My own business! That's a great idea!" Jeffrey shouts.

"Let's brainstorm," says Jasmine.

Jeffrey goes to his desk and finds a notepad and a pencil. He begins to write down some ideas:

* walk neighbors' dogs
* bake cookies
* run errands

* sell lemonade

* wash cars

* mow lawns

Suddenly, Jeffrey's face lights up! He knows just which project to take on! Jasmine begs to be a part, too. She loves to bake, and Jeffrey knows his friends are always thirsty. Jeffrey has $10 in his bank. He thinks of a plan to present to his parents.

*   *   *

It's 2:45 p.m. on a Saturday afternoon. The community meeting starts at 3 p.m. and the committee that Jeffrey spearheads with Victor must present. Everyone will be anxious to hear what recommendations the team has come up with. Like the other families, the Woods arrive at the community center on time. They hope the meeting will be short.

Mayor Vandyke calls the meeting to order. He asks the Community Concerns Committee to come to the front to share their recommendations about the video games problem. The fifth graders want to present, and Jeffrey agrees. Everyone listens very carefully to the suggestions. Every family likes the idea of a new team captain each week. Some of the children pout when the committee recommends that they read a book before playing video games. Overall, the committee's suggestions are received and approved by the community. Everyone seems pleased and leaves the Community Center without an argument, a copy of the guidelines in hand.

Jeffrey and the committee sigh together, "Whew, it's over!"

Now that this project is behind him, Jeffrey can finally focus on his own concerns.

*   *   *

At 3:30 p.m., the Woods family is back home, and Jeffrey and Jasmine rush to his bedroom. They estimate that one hour and 50 minutes will be just enough time to outline plans for starting a business.

While he has the nerve and Jasmine's support, Jeffrey- with Jasmine behind him—goes to the kitchen to find their parents.

It's 5:20 p.m., and their mom and dad are talking and laughing while he is preparing Saturday dinner, with a hand from her.

The aroma of fresh herbs, tomato sauce, and cheese fills the house. To Jeffrey's and Jasmine's surprise, their dad has pulled together all the ingredients to make their favorite dish: lasagna!

"Dinner will be served in about 40 minutes," Dad announces as Jeffrey and Jasmine enter the kitchen. "What are the two of you up to?" Dad asks.

Without thinking, Jeffrey says, "Nothing." He quickly clears his throat, "Can we talk?"

Both parents look curiously at each other, waiting to hear what their son is about to say, but Jeffrey freezes.

"Let the lightning flash before us!" Dad declares with great drama. "Are you volunteering to take out the trash for the next nine weeks? Or are you volunteering to wash your mom's and my car every weekend?"

Jeffrey relaxes. "Dad, the schedule works as it is, thank you! I want to talk to you and Mom about how I haven't been spending my allowance responsibly."

Dad and Mom look at each other in amazement.

Jeffrey takes a deep breath. "I'm not expecting more money from you, but I have come up with a plan to earn extra money. If you decide it's a good one, you can help with it."

Mom asks, "What do you need the money for?"

"I've seen this watch that I really, really, really like," Jeffrey says. "I desperately want it! I've never seen anything like it! My plan is to set up a cookie and lemonade stand as a business. Jasmine wants to be my partner."

Dad ponders Jeffrey's remarks for a few minutes. "Your mom and I need to discuss this new venture. We're glad to hear you own up to squandering your allowance. Perhaps, you're beginning to understand what it means to be responsible."

I'm beginning to get the picture," Jeffrey replies.

CHAPTER 5

Feeling the Heat

Dinner is now 20 minutes away. With a nod toward the living room, Jasmine beckons to Jeffrey. She compliments her brother on the good job he has done in presenting his plan.

Jasmine nervously refers to an important day. "You know what is going to happen next Sunday."

"What?" Jeffrey responds with aggravation, without noticing his tone.

"JEFFrey!" Jasmine says hurtfully.

He quickly uses a softer tone, "Grandma and Granddaddy are coming to visit!"

Jasmine nods yes.

"Let's retrace your steps," Jeffrey suggests. "Let's look at everything, and find where the gap is. What happened after the piano recital?"

"You remember. We went out to celebrate. Grandma, Granddaddy, Mom, and Dad were pleased, and so was I. We went to the Kool, the new ice cream parlor. It was gigantic! I had a large sundae with two scoops of vanilla ice cream and a lot of toppings. It was so good!"

"Jasmine, get to the point!" interrupts Jeffrey.

Refusing to be distracted, Jasmine pauses. "We came home, and Grandma mentioned how tired she was and thought it was a good idea to get some sleep. Granddaddy agreed, and they went to bed. That was about 9:30 p.m. You and I stayed up talking for about 30 minutes. I started to yawn, and you said, 'Let's get some zzzs.'"

Jasmine focuses and rushes, talking faster. "The next day I checked to see if I had put the necklace in the jewelry chest. It was there. The rest of the weekend was filled with listening to Grandma and Granddaddy share amazing stories about Mom when she was a kid. It was so funny to find out interesting things about her.

Grandma asked to see the necklace, taking a picture of it with her new smart phone because she wanted to buy the matching bracelet, which was on sale at Kacy Department Store."

Jasmine stops for a moment, then recalls, "Mom volunteered to take Grandma to the store. While they were getting ready to leave, Sylvia Scott popped her head through the doorway and asked me to come to see her new . . . ."

"Anyone who knows Sylvia *knows* she loves dolls," Jeffrey adds.

"May I finish?" Jasmine asks, annoyed. "She saw Grandma's necklace in my hand and said how nice it was. It was so obvious that Sylvia was anxious for me to see her new doll. She rushed me out of the door to her house."

"You were flying past me," Jeffrey says. "As I was coming in, you shouted for me to tell Mom that you were going next door."

Jasmine starts laughing.

"Jasmine, you're messing up! Stay focused."

"Okay, I'll focus. I held the necklace very tightly in my hand. When I got to Sylvia's room and saw the new doll, I couldn't believe how beautiful she looked. I got a tingling feeling when I put the necklace around the doll's neck. The pearl has a shiny glow. Sylvia and I played with her dolls until Mom called. Grandma and Granddaddy wanted to leave before dark, so I quickly said goodbye to Sylvia."

Jasmine catches her breath. "From Sylvia's house, I ran as fast as I could to see Grandma and Granddaddy before they got in the car. I wanted to kiss them goodbye."

"Jasmine, your *problemo* is solved!" boasts Jeffrey. "The necklace is around the new doll's neck!"

"Hold on, Jeffrey, that's not quite where it is. Sylvia's little sister, Genet, loves dolls, too. Without permission, Genet took Sylvia's new doll when she went on errands with her dad. When she put the doll back in Sylvia's room, the necklace wasn't on the doll. Genet can't remember if she saw a necklace on the doll."

"It seems as though someone is in hot water."

"Ouch!" says Jasmine. "Solving this problem means having other people retrace their steps. Who do I ask? Where do I start?"

Jeffrey reminds her that she has little time—seven days to be exact—to discover more clues.

CHAPTER 6

Dealing With Twists and Turns

Sylvia's dad and 5-year-old Genet are backing the car out of the driveway to go shopping for the family. Genet doesn't know Jasmine has come over to see her big sister. Right now, she's in charge of the things-to-do list. She is pleased with her assigned task and the company she brings with her: the doll.

The errands are listed in order of importance, starting with pricing the ceiling fan, checking the cost of a tall ladder, and buying one pack of 60-watt light bulbs. The list has grown to include a stop at the grocery store for a large tomato, three large cucumbers, and a head of romaine lettuce.

When they reach the first destination, Philip Scott opens the door for his daughter. "Genet, leave the doll in the car," he says.

"Daddy, I wanna take the doll!" Genet whines and pouts. She scoots off her seat, twisting and turning her tiny body until she is on the car floor. Her eyes fill up with tears. To keep her happy, the doll comes along every place they travel.

Genet skips down the aisle at Tru-Home Store. While talking to a salesperson about the ceiling fan, Mr. Scott keeps an eye on his daughter. But Genet always finds a way to do what she wants, even when she's been told not to.

"Don't touch any of the lamps, Genet," her dad warns gently.

She is fascinated by the variety! There's a paper balloon lampshade shaped like a real balloon and dangling from a long, arched, silver pole. She closely examines a lamp pole that looks like a tree with three bell-shaped, miniature lanterns.

Genet sighs in wonder as she clicks on each light. She peers at two different colored lamps with Asian peacock scenes painted on the bases and crowned with diamond-shaped lampshades. She giggles as she dances the doll on top of different lampshades.

"I told you not to touch anything, Genet! Come here!" her dad says, using a firmer tone.

As father and daughter head to the appliance department, Genet skips and turns a cartwheel. "Genet, you're not at cheerleading practice," Mr. Scott reminds her. "Let's *walk* to the next place."

Genet nods her head, gazing with her big brown eyes. "Yes, Daddy, I can walk."

They continue to the ladder section, where Mr. Scott immediately finds another salesperson. Looking into his daughter's eyes, he cautions her, "Genet, don't play on the ladder."

"Yes, Daddy, I won't play."

Still, Mr. Scott knows he has to watch his little girl, who is constantly in motion.

Genet is amazed when she sees three ladders arranged from the shortest to the tallest. She looks around to see if her dad is watching her but decides he's too busy to do that. Mr. Scott needs to purchase a ladder for the projects his wife has been asking him to do. Still, he watches Genet out of the corners of his eyes. She maneuvers the doll to jump each step of the shortest ladder until it reaches the top of the ladder. After mastering this challenge, Genet beams with confidence. Then, on the second tallest ladder, she reasons that she has to stand on the bottom step to get the doll to the top. She is triumphant and twirls and bounces the doll in the air!

She lets out a melodious, "Weee!" Now, on her third and final challenge, she moves to the tallest ladder. This one is much harder and higher for her to manage each step of the doll to the top of the ladder.

Genet's dad stops his conversation with the salesperson, turns, and warns his daughter with a raised voice. "Genet, DON'T PLAY ON THAT LADDER!"

Mr. Scott picks up the conversation with the sales associate, giving Genet the opportunity to ignore his order again. While leaning against the ladder, she tiptoes and loses her balance. With a mighty swing, she throws her doll to the top of the ladder. It almost reaches the top but begins to tumble, performing three somersaults before the necklace falls off. Her dad catches her before she falls, but he doesn't notice the necklace.

As she pulls herself together, Genet sees where the necklace has landed. She quickly scoops it up off the floor and puts it in her pocket, not saying a single word to her dad about it. Genet knows she's in trouble. Looking at her dad with faked innocence, she whispers, "Uh, oh!"

"Uh, oh is right!" her dad says firmly. "For the rest of the errands, you have to pretend that you're a robot and can only move when you get directions."

After Mr. Scott prices the ladder, he decides to wait for it to go on sale and to buy the light bulbs another time. Purchasing the ceiling fan, a great deal, and on sale for 50% off was needed. Genet walks like a robot to get in the car.

Mr. Scott checks the to-do list—left in the car tray compartment—to determine where to go next. This errand is closer to home. When they reach the grocery store—their last stop—he reminds his daughter, "Genet, you are a robot. Robots must follow directions."

"I am a robot!" she mimics. In her robotic state, Genet and the doll accompany her dad into the store. Since everything on the list is in the same section, they shop with ease. To Mr. Scott's surprise, the express lane moves quickly. He pays for the items, picks up his bag, and leaves the store, placing the groceries on the floor behind the driver's seat.

On the way home, Genet's dad turns on Sunnyside Street, right near the Kool Ice Cream Parlor. He hears Genet making little noises and sees in the mirror that she is twisting around in her seat belt. She points to the parlor and whines loudly, "I want an ice cream cone!"

"Genet, your favorite ice cream is at home," he reminds her.

Suddenly, one of his co-workers, Kyle Goldstein—who has a son the same age as Genet—pulls into the parlor's parking lot. Mr. Scott has wanted to talk to him, and this may be just the right moment. There's nothing at home that needs immediate attention, so he heads for a parking space on the crowded lot. Genet joyfully claps her hands and lets out an enthusiastic "Yay!" But Mr. Scott notices his daughter acting strangely, twisting from one hip to the other. "Genet, is something wrong?"

Smiling at him, she says, "No, Daddy, nothing's wrong." But she realizes that the necklace in her pocket is bothering her. She needs to put it someplace. As her dad is getting out of the car, she slips it into the grocery bag. Mr. Scott walks around to open the door on her side. She gets out, looks back, and grabs the doll to take it with her into the ice cream parlor.

The timing for meeting another coworker at the ice cream parlor is amazing. Philip has been trying to meet with Kyle to discuss how they could form a team for an organization-wide project. As the dads brainstorm, their children enjoy ice cream and look forward to playing on the slides. Genet skips a few feet from the slides, catches her dad's expression, and moves back to the play area. The dads wrap up their conversation, and Genet grabs the doll to leave.

After the errands and the short ice cream escapade, Dad and a sleepy Genet are five minutes from home.

CHAPTER 7

Holding His Breath for the Big Decision

At the Woods' house, Jeffrey is pondering how to get his parents' decision about starting his own business. It's one minute before dinner. Jeffrey and Jasmine surprise their parents and show up without being called several times.

Dinner is on the table, and Jeffrey observes that his dad is in a very good mood. Jasmine piles up her plate with her favorite vegetable and then adds the main entrée: lasagna. She crunches on a crisp salad made of spinach leaves mixed with romaine lettuce, cherry tomatoes, red bell peppers, sliced mushrooms, and diced onions, all tossed with her favorite Ranch dressing. In the middle of the meal, Dad asks Jasmine to sound off a bugle fanfare. He has a surprise announcement. Jeffrey braces himself for the decision he's hoping for.

"Who do you know has been reading stories at the Children's Center at the hospital?"

Jasmine and Jeffrey answer in unison, "Mom!"

"I am pleased to announce that your mom has been selected to serve as the new chairperson of the Children's Book Drive," Dad explains proudly. "A member of the committee has called to let your mom know that her hard work has been appreciated. They feel she is the best chairperson for this noteworthy project."

"I'm stunned but delighted to hear their surprising decision," says Mom.

Dad's good news lingers in the room. Finally catching Jeffrey's eye, Jasmine whispers, "Do it now!"

After mounding another big scoop of lasagna on his plate, Jeffrey decorates it with a gigantic salad. He savors each bite of the lasagna and tells his dad how tasty it is. At last, he summons enough courage and clears his throat to say, "Dad, what thoughts do you and Mom have about allowing me to open a lemonade and cookie stand?"

His dad looks at his wife and asks her to announce their decision. Jeffrey's mom hesitates in a playful manner and happily says, "Yes, you may!"

Jeffrey is thrilled! He and Jasmine do a high five as she chimes, "That's so cool!"

"I'd like to find out how Jasmine and I can help Mom with the book drive," Jeffrey says.

"That's a good idea," Dad says. "We can discuss your ideas for your project over dessert. I almost forgot to tell you that your mom and I thought you and the committee did a good job with the video games recommendations and setting a schedule for making them a part of family entertainment."

Jasmine jumps up from the table, springs into a cheerleading stunt, and yells, "You go, Jeffrey!"

Amazed at Jasmine's exuberance, Mom raises her eyebrows and shakes her head with a laugh. "Miss Bubbly, please sit down and finish your dinner. Let's hope your brother and you can keep this magical feeling while doing your favorite chore: washing the dishes."

After dinner, Jeffrey and Jasmine clean the kitchen and finish their assigned chores. Jasmine tags along with Jeffrey to his room. He takes out his notepad and begins to jot down his ideas. Jasmine adds her suggestions. There are a lot of events going on in the park. Jeffrey will pass out flyers, announcing the service he will be providing to the neighborhood at the park events.

He determines who his potential customers will be:

* sports teams and fans
* neighborhood friends
* club members
* school friends

Jeffrey lists the ingredients needed to make the lemonade: sugar, water, lemons, and limes. They'll also need paper cups (12 oz. and 20 oz.), napkins, and a large ice cooler or a large container. Jasmine comes up with the ingredients she'll need for baking the cookies: sugar, flour, salt, baking powder, vanilla flavor, dark brown sugar, eggs, margarine, chocolate chips, and pecans.

She has no doubt that her cookies will sell; she bakes the best cookies in town—under her mom's watchful eye. Jasmine proudly reminds Jeffrey that she has won a blue ribbon for her cookies at the Somerville Community Center Bazaar. She knows that the special watch he wants so badly costs $75.

Jeffrey figures that a major sporting event at the neighborhood park attracts as many as 180 people. He calculates the number of cups he would have to sell. The two popular cup sizes are 12 ounces and 20 ounces. Of course, for his event to be successful, he has to determine what each cup size would cost. Later, he'll set up a chart to show the different ways he can reach his sales goal.

All the neighbors love Jasmine's famous cookies! She estimates the number of cookies to bake. The sale of the cookies will help pay one-third of the cost of the watch Jeffrey so desperately wants. She thinks the cookies will sell faster if they are priced five for $1. Jasmine has to calculate how much money she will make. To determine how many cookies must be sold to reach the goal, Jasmine begins drawing a chart.

Calculating out loud, Jasmine says, "If I sell . . ."

Jasmine is so absorbed in Jeffrey's plan that she almost forgets her own dilemma. She loses her concentration for figuring out how many cookies she must sell, and her thoughts begin to drift. Jeffrey notices the change and decides that the chart can be done later.

"Jasmine, are you thinking about the necklace Grandma gave you?" he asks slowly.

Jeffrey immediately stops what he is doing and devotes his time to helping his sister retrace her steps.

"If I remember correctly, Genet couldn't recall seeing the necklace at all on the doll."

"That, that's correct," Jasmine stammers.

"Jasmine, the necklace will turn up," Jeffrey reassures her. "I have an idea. Ask Sylvia to check Genet's bedroom for the necklace. Check her clothes. Ask her to retrace Genet's steps as best she can."

Jasmine perks up a bit after hearing Jeffrey's advice and agrees to talk to Sylvia on Monday before class.

CHAPTER 8

Getting on the Case

On Monday, Sylvia and Jasmine talk. Sylvia promises to get back to Jasmine in a couple of days. But by Wednesday, Jasmine has not heard from her best friend, so she decides to risk calling her. She knows Sylvia's parents could be within earshot and discover what their conversation is about, but her prayer is answered when Sylvia answers the phone.

"Sylvia, I haven't heard from you. What did you find out?"

"I'm sorry! I forgot to call to let you know that I've retraced all the steps Genet could remember, but she can't recall what happened to the necklace. I don't know what to say Jasmine! I wish I had good news."

"Hey, have your privileges been stopped because of video games?" Sylvia asks, changing the subject. "My parents plan to follow the suggestions your brother and the committee came up with."

"My dad complimented Jeffrey for the good job the committee did," Jasmine says. "The message is: As long as you work together and follow the guidelines, privileges are rewarded."

"There *is* something we can learn from the community meeting!" Sylvia says. They both laugh.

Jasmine agrees as she sees the humor that Sylvia hints at. "Absolutely."

"Sylvia, what time next Saturday would be good to work on our science project?" asks Jasmine, switching the subject again. "I'm so excited to work on this project with you. It should be fun sharing facts about the Milky Way with the rest of the class. This could be the beginning of us becoming astronomers!"

"It's in our destiny to reach for the stars!" says Sylvia, and they both laugh.

Suddenly, Sylvia remembers the last place her sister has been. "It was the family car!" she blurts. "I don't believe this! Dad has gone to check on his uncle and won't return until the weekend!"

"Maybe there's still hope," says Jasmine.

"Let's wait and see," Sylvia says calmly.

She promises her friend that she won't forget to check the car as soon as her dad returns.

CHAPTER 9

Hoping for a Miracle

On Saturday afternoon, Sylvia's dad returns from visiting his uncle. As he enters the house, Mr. Scott sees his daughters, who greet him with a kiss. He tells them how pleased he is to find that his uncle shows a lot of spunk and grit as he recovers from surgery. As he moves toward the living room his wife, Vanessa, rushes to greet him with a big hug and to find out the news about his uncle.

While Sylvia stands in the front door, she notices that her dad has left his small overnight bag in the car, which is parked in the driveway. She grabs the keys from the tray on the table in the living room and heads to the car, but finds that the doors are still unlocked.

Sylvia mumbles to herself, "This is a perfect time to look for the necklace!" She opens the car door and pokes her fingers between the tight and narrow places in the cushions of the front seats, then checks beneath them.

"Whew, this is hard!" she pants. "It must be in the back." She opens the back door, crawls onto the seat, and leans forward to extend her hands under the passenger and driver seats. Then she swirls her body around squeezing her fingers to check the tight places of the back seat cushion.

After a lot of poking and prodding, she comes up exhausted. The only thing she finds is the missing pen from the writing set she got last Christmas.

"I don't believe this! There's nothing here!" she sighs in dismay.

Sylvia closes the car door and ends her search for the necklace.

She starts to leave, but decides to check the trunk. It's the last resort. Just maybe. But the last glimmer of hope disappointingly reveals nothing.

She tells her dad that she found the car unlocked and took the keys to lock it. "Thanks for being so observant, Honey!" he says.

Now, Sylvia hears her parents discussing the news about her dad's uncle in their bedroom. Genet decides to watch her favorite TV show in *her* bedroom. This is the ideal time! The kitchen is the best place to call Jasmine and report the results of her search. She knows her friend is expecting to hear good news, so she dials Jasmine's telephone number. The phone barely rings twice when Sylvia hears Jasmine's voice on the other end.

"Hello!" says Jasmine.

"Hello, Jasmine, hello! I surprised you. I didn't forget to get back to you."

"What did you find?" Jasmine asks nervously.

"There's no sign of the necklace in the car," says Sylvia, reluctantly. "It's not there. I'm sorry!"

They hold the phone without speaking, knowing that any ray of sunshine seems to have dimmed.

"Again, I'm sorry that the news isn't good. I'll talk to you later."

"Thanks, Sylvia! Bye!" says Jasmine.

Digesting the news that Sylvia shared, Jasmine releases a sigh of frustration. "What can I do to get out of this hot water?"

CHAPTER 10

It's Getting Hotter

As Jeffrey passes his little sister's doorway, he hears an outburst. Jeffrey pops his head inside and says, "What's going on, Pumpkin? The look on your face tells me that the news isn't good."

"I just talked to Sylvia. She couldn't find the necklace. I can't believe this!" Jasmine says, frantically.

"Whoa, Jas! I know everything is going to get better. Just hold on! We're going to come up with a solution. Wanna play a game of Chinese checkers?"

"You know how to get me smiling again," says Jasmine.

Jeffrey knows in his heart that—instead of using the money from the cookies and lemonade sales for his watch—he must devise a way to buy another necklace. He also knows that Jasmine will object. This reality—his secret—is something he can't share with her.

Jeffrey's frustration with his sister's dilemma becomes an anchor for him. It evolves as something that has to be faced, and he affirms, repeating several times: "The solution will be difficult, but it can be achieved. You gotta do what you gotta do!"

CHAPTER 11

Figuring It Out

As Sylvia ends her conversation on the phone with Jasmine, her mom interrupts her husband's conversation about his uncle's recovery and says, "Before I forget, I found something in the bag after Genet and you returned from doing errands." She shows him the pearl necklace.

"When Genet and I were on our way home from the ice cream parlor, she became sleepy, gave the doll to me, and I put it in the grocery bag," Mr. Scott says. "She didn't mention anything about a necklace. I wonder who it belongs to?"

"I think I know whose it is," says Mrs. Scott. "Let's see! Genet loves to wear colored barrettes and headbands to match her outfits, and Sylvia's favorite jewelry is bracelets."

"Well, while you're trying to figure out who it belongs to, I want to do something before watching the history documentary I told you about. Let's look at it in the family room. I'll be right back."

Mr. Scott goes into the kitchen to prepare a different kind of snack from his usual steak and cheese sandwich. He checks the refrigerator and discovers a tray of crisp vegetables with carrots, celery, and broccoli. He then looks in the cabinet for his favorite dip but can't find it. It's got to be there! His wife, Vanessa, has organized the four-shelf pantry a certain way: baking items such as flour, cornmeal, sugar, salt, and fish-fry seasoning on top; all the cereals on the second shelf; canned vegetables on the third; and snacks—potato chips, pretzels, peanut butter, crackers, and his favorite dip—on the fourth shelf. His impromptu hunch could prevent him from being on time for the documentary. He quickly changes his strategy and checks the kitchen counter. There it is! He grabs the vegetables and dip and rushes to the family room.

Mrs. Scott continues thinking out loud. "Sylvia's friend, Marcy, likes to wear earrings, but not bracelets or necklaces." After considering whose necklace it could be, she reaches a conclusion. "That leaves only one girl who is always in and out of this house."

Sylvia's dad and mom sit down to watch the documentary together, munching on the delicious snack.

"I need to return some items to Liz Woods, so I'll put the necklace in an envelope and take it with me," says Mrs. Scott to her husband.

"Shhhh!" he says. "The show's about to start."

CHAPTER 12

The Eleventh Hour Arrives

It's Sunday afternoon, and Jasmine knows the clock is counting down. Her grandparents will arrive before dusk. In her bedroom, she practices what she'll say to her mom about losing her grandma's necklace. It will be a relief when the dreaded dilemma ends.

Meanwhile, Jeffrey gets a call from Victor, who wants to go to the mall. He needs Jeffrey's opinion about some basketball gear he wants to buy. "Good idea," says Jeffrey. Jeffrey agrees to go but must get permission from his dad. This will give him the chance to look at the watch, but he has to be back before his grandparents arrive.

Jeffrey is waiting on the porch when Victor and his dad arrive. At the mall, Jeffrey offers his advice but Victor still can't quite make up his mind.

"I might not know what I want to buy, but I do know who's in!" teases Victor.

"Now, you're the joker!" says Jeffrey. "Who's in what? Do I have to stand on my head to get you to tell me what's going on?"

"Yeah, stand on your head!" Victor challenges. "No, I'm just kidding. I've been accepted in the Math Club."

"Yeah, me too!" says Jeffrey. "It's great news! We all finally heard something."

"Victor, take your time, and get what you like. Then Marcus, Andre, and I will not have to listen to another one of your 'I-wish-I had-this-stories," Jeffrey jokes.

"Yeah, OK!" Victor says. "Go look at your watch!"

"I'll be back in a flash, and—*hopefully*—you'll have made up your mind," says Jeffrey, as he speeds off.

When he gets to the store, Jeffrey flashes a smile at the pleasant salesperson who assisted him before and looks at his special watch.

*   *   *

Jasmine's butterflies are fluttering at high speed. She looks everywhere but can't find Jeffrey. She shakes herself. "Brace up! It's time to tell Mom. This is the most awful thing in my life! Where's Jeffrey?"

Enduring several short, frenzied moments, she begins to fidget with the items on her dresser: a collection of jewelry, little treasures, and necessities she has carefully arranged to reflect her flair for decoration. Now, nothing looks right. In a burst of nerves, she clears everything off the dresser to position them differently. She rearranges the necklaces hanging on her jewelry tree, swapping the key pendant with the dangling teddy bear. Then she changes her mind and moves her prized cheerleading necklace to another branch. She even moves the heart-shaped musical box where the missing pearl necklace is supposed to be to the spot always occupied by her oval mirror. She struggles to get a grip on herself.

She finally freezes when she imagines her grandma's disappointed face, and she buries her own face in her hands. Jasmine struggles not to fall apart. She tries to focus on the astronomy project and writes down a few ideas. Her jitters come and go as she agonizes and moves much slower than usual. She doesn't want to face what she knows is coming.

As she takes her time going to her mom in the kitchen, she hears the doorbell and then a knock on the door. Her heart beats faster.

"That can't be my grandparents," she mumbles to herself. "They shouldn't be here for another two hours." She slowly opens the door and is relieved to see Sylvia's mother, Mrs. Scott.

"Jasmine, Sylvia and I are on our way out, but I had to stop to return these items to your mother," says Mrs. Scott, as she places a bag into Jasmine's hands. "Tell her thanks, and I'll call her later."

Jasmine lacks enthusiasm. Just then the telephone rings. She has a hunch that it's her grandparents. It's confirmed when her mother says, "OK, Mom, take your time. Drive safely, now."

After she hangs up, Jasmine's mom notices the look on her daughter's face and asks, "What's going on?"

"Everything's OK," Jasmine replies, squinting her face.

"How about baking those delicious cookies for dessert? I'm sure your grandparents will enjoy them."

"That's a great idea, Mom!"

Jasmine carefully moves a small stepladder to the kitchen cabinets and starts gathering ingredients. Although she knows this recipe by heart, she wants to make sure she hasn't left anything out. She thoughtfully recalls what her mom has taught her about checking to see if she has what she needs to get the job done. Once she grabs the salt, a teaspoon, a large spoon, and the mixer, she's ready.

Jasmine's mom returns to the kitchen after completing a household task. "Good job, Jas!" her mother acknowledges. "OK, Honey! Get the mixing bowl and the large spoon. Put one of the sticks of margarine in the mixing bowl and break it into smaller pieces with the big spoon. Then, repeat the same steps with the other stick of margarine," instructs her mom.

Jasmine expresses her readiness, "Mom, I remember how to do this."

As a review, her mom cautions her about how to cream the margarine in the mixing bowl. She signals her daughter to switch places, allowing her to begin the process.

"See how I'm taking time to cream the margarine?" her mom asks.

"Mom, may I do it?"

Within seconds, they trade places again so that Jasmine can complete this step.

"So, what do we do next, Jasmine?"

"Mix in the sugar! I like that part." Jasmine tilts the measuring cup with the sugar and watches it descend with a sparkle. Then she carefully grips the big spoon to blend the sugar and the margarine into a completely different texture.

"Jasmine, may I finish the stirring, using the mixer?"

Jasmine nods her head. "Yes, you can." She adds, "I've forgotten how to crack the eggs," says Jasmine.

"I can save you there," says her mom, smiling.

She cracks one egg, then another, which open like parachutes. As they drop quickly, they change the landscape of the ingredients in the bowl. Jasmine stirs them into the mixture, altering the texture even more.

"Now, we can add the rest of the ingredients," says Mom. "You do some, and I'll do some." They take turns pouring the flour, salt, baking powder, and vanilla flavor transforming the mixture even more. Jasmine closes her eyes and breathes in the sweet aroma of cookie dough.

"Mom, we can't forget to add the chocolate chips and pecans."

"You're absolutely right! We can't forget the best part."

The last thing is for Jasmine to roll the cookie dough into ping-pong-size balls. Then she molds them into flat rounds, places them onto the cookie sheet, and—with her mother's help—slides them into the hot oven.

By the time all the cookies are done, the scrumptious smell of chocolate fills the house. "Congratulations, Sweetie! You've done a good job. Your grandparents will love these."

"Thanks, Mom! We're a good team!"

Time seems to have passed quickly, and her grandparents will arrive soon.

CHAPTER 13

From Dreaded to the Unexpected

By 3:30 p.m., Jeffrey hasn't called or shown up. "He knows he has to call home to let Mom and Dad know where he is," Jasmine grumbles to herself. "More than likely, he's playing basketball with his friends. All good things must come to an end."

Jasmine sighs and thinks how she has enjoyed baking with her mom. To delay confessing the fate of the necklace, Jasmine's eyes spot the items that Sylvia's mother has brought back. They're still on the counter.

"Mom, do you want me to put these things away?"

"That would be nice, Honey!"

As Jasmine reaches for the items, she faintly hears a car horn. Her mom looks out of the living room window and sees her parents. "Jasmine, finish putting the things away, and then come greet your grandparents."

Jasmine thinks over and over to herself, "Why didn't I tell Mom about the necklace?" realizing that she didn't have the nerve. She then wonders, "*Where* is *Jeffrey?*"

Suddenly, she hears her brother offering to help their grandparents with their bags. Jasmine continues putting away the things in the kitchen and comes down to the last item: an unmarked envelope. "What could it be?"

The car doors slam. The moment has come for Jasmine to face her grandma. "This is it!" she sighs, trying to slow down her pounding heart. In a final effort to delay the inevitable, she gives in to her curiosity and rips open the white envelope. Her eyes fill with tears of relief as she sees the iridescent gleam inside. The necklace! She is surprised and stunned beyond disbelief, but quickly recovers. She could scream, but works to remain calm.

Within a few minutes her grandparents enter the house. "Smells like *somebody's* been baking?" says Granddaddy.

"That's *got* to be Jasmine's famous chocolate chip cookies!" says Grandma.

Everyone laughs as Jasmine enters the living room, but Jeffrey's laugh melts into a fretful look. He tries to think of something to help his sister in her moment of desperation. Suddenly, he blurts out, "Grandma and Granddaddy, I have something to tell you. Jasmine and I are going into business together. That way she'll be able to replace your neck . . . ."

Jasmine abruptly interrupts Jeffrey. "Grandma, I think Jeffrey is trying to tell you something about the necklace, my necklace."

Grandma looks puzzled and turns to Jeffrey. "What about the necklace?"

Immediately, Jasmine confidently says, "What Jeffrey means is that I want to *place* the necklace around your neck."

Jasmine opens her hand and shows the necklace. "This will look so pretty with what you're wearing."

Jeffrey is stunned but pleased.

"Yes, that's what I meant to say," says Jeffrey. "Jasmine wants to place this lovely necklace around the neck of the lovely person who always does lovely things for others." Jasmine laughs nervously as Jeffrey recovers from a near blunder.

As they all embrace each other, Grandma says to their mom and dad, "Somehow there is more to this situation than what meets the eye, but we'll discuss it later."

CHAPTER 14

Moving Ahead

"Jeffrey, where have you been?" asks Jasmine.

"I went to the department store to look at the watch."

"Are we still on with the neighborhood business?"

Jeffrey lets out a sigh of relief. "Now that your dilemma is solved, we can work to get the business started and finish writing our sales projections. As a team, we have a good chance."

"It's on, big brother!"

"Yeah, but there's other work I've still gotta do," Jeffrey says, acting on a detective hunch. "A new family has moved into the Johnson's house on Neighbor Lane. Look what I found on the ground next to their mailbox."

He reaches into his pocket, pulls out a small video game, and the two burst into laughter. "I guess I'll have to pay them a welcome-to-the-neighborhood visit!"

—End—